Hannah is sixteen and lives on an island. She is on holiday from school and is working for Mr Duval on his glass-bottomed boat. They take people to look at the beautiful fish and the coral reef under the sea. Mr Duval can only pay Hannah a little money, but she likes working for the old man. Mr Duval's boat is the only glass-bottomed boat on the island. But one day...

"Look, Mr Duval!" says Hannah. "There's a new glass-bottomed boat!" Hannah is right. The new boat is taking people out to look at the coral reef, and there are people waiting for it to come back.

"Why are all the people going on the new boat and not on my boat?" says Mr Duval. "What's happening?"

"I'm going to find out," says Hannah.

Hannah soon has the answer. "It's cheaper!" she says.
"Yes," says a man standing behind her. "And it's going
to be the *only* glass-bottomed boat on the island in a
month or two. It's going to be 'Goodbye, Mr Duval!'"
And he laughs. Hannah knows the man. His name is
Max Marker. He is very rich and has a big house on the
island. "Is it your boat?" she asks. "Yes," he says.

"Why is it cheaper on your boat?" Hannah asks. "Oh, I know!" she says, "you want to stop Mr Duval's boat and then your prices can go up." Max smiles. "Come and work for me," he says. "I can pay you lots of money." "No," says Hannah. "I like working for Mr Duval. Money isn't everything." "You're wrong," says Max. He is laughing again, but it is not a nice laugh.

The weeks go by. People do not come to Mr Duval's
boat. "I'm sorry, but there is no more work for you,
Hannah," says Mr Duval one day. "It's OK," says
Hannah, but she is very sad to lose her job.
Max goes to see the old man. "Do you want to sell your
boat?" he asks. "I can give you a good price for it." Mr
Duval is very angry. "No!" he says.

The next morning Mr Duval goes to his boat – and sees that it is under the water! "Oh no!" he says. "I don't understand."

Hannah comes later that morning. The radio says there is a strong storm coming – a hurricane! She wants to help Mr Duval get his boat into the boathouse. But now she sees the glass-bottomed boat under the water.

"This is Max Marker's work!" says Hannah. "He wants to destroy your business." "I'm an old man," says Mr Duval. "I'm too tired to fight Max Marker and his nasty games." "I'm not!" says Hannah. "I'm going to his house to see him!"

But it is too late. The hurricane is coming! "We must get to my house!" says Mr Duval.

The hurricane hits the island at 11 o'clock that morning.
It pulls trees from the ground and they crash down on
houses. Cars roll across the road like children's toys.
Soon, many of the island's roads are under water! The
strong wind throws Max Marker's boat out of the water,
and against a wall. Hannah and Mr Duval are safe in a
room under the old man's house.

The hurricane goes on for four hours. Slowly, the wind gets weaker and weaker. Two hours later, people start to come out of their houses. The rain stops.

"Now I can go to see Max Marker about his nasty games," says Hannah. "What can you do?" says Mr Duval. "How can you stop him?" "I don't know," says Hannah, angrily. "But I can do *something!*" And she runs off.

Hannah goes to Max Marker's big house. She sees the
work of the hurricane. Some of his house is gone!
"Where is Max Marker?" she thinks. "Is he inside?" She
starts to run to the house, but she is afraid.
Max Marker *is* inside the house – and he cannot get
out! "Help! Help!" he says. "I'm going to die!" But the
wind takes his words and carries them away.

Hannah can hear Max Marker but she cannot see him.
"Where are you?" she says. "Here!" he says. "I'm over
here!" Suddenly, she sees him.
"He's not laughing now," she thinks. There are stones
and some of the roof on top of him.
"Help me!" he cries. "Please!"
"I'm coming," she tells him.

Hannah climbs across and starts to pull the stones off
him. It is not easy. The stones are very heavy. She gets
one off him . . . then the next one . . . "Faster!" he tells her,
"Work faster!" "I – I can't!" she cries.

Suddenly, there is a noise above her. Hannah looks up –
some of the roof is coming down!

"Help!" says Max, and he starts to cry.

Hannah jumps away and the roof crashes down near
her. She waits for ten seconds, and she can see again.
She climbs back across the stones to Max Marker. He is
very happy to see her!

"How long before *all* the house comes down?" thinks
Hannah. "Can I get him out quickly?" She starts to
work faster.

Max can move now but he is very weak. He stands up slowly, then he climbs out of the house. Hannah helps him across the street. They look back. The house crashes to the ground!

But Max Marker is smiling now. "You're very brave," he says, "thank you, my friend."

"I'm *not* your friend," says Hannah.

"How can I pay you?" says Max. "Pay for Mr Duval's boat," says Hannah. "And stop your nasty games! Work together with the two boats. Don't fight." "OK," says Max Marker, "but what can I give *you*?" "I don't want anything," says Hannah. "Some money?" asks Max. "No, thank you," says Hannah. "Money isn't every-thing." "Yes, I'm starting to understand that," says Max.

ACTIVITIES

Before you read

1 Look at the Word List at the back of the book. What are the words in
   your language?

2 Read the questions and talk to a friend.

   a   What do you know about hurricanes?

   b   How many islands do you know?

3 Look at the pictures in the book and answer the questions.

   a   Page 1. What is Hannah doing in the old man's boat?

   b   Page 1. Why are the visitors looking down?

   c   Page 2. How much is a ticket to the coral reef?

   d   Pages 3 and 4. Is the man rich or not rich?

While you read

4 Read pages 1–5. Are the sentences right (✓) or wrong (✗)?

   a   Hannah is seventeen.   .....

   b   She likes her job with old Mr Duval.   .....

   c   There are three glass-bottomed boats on the island.   .....

   d   Tickets for the big new boat are cheap.   .....

   e   Many visitors come to Mr Duval's boat.   .....

   f   Hannah doesn't want a job with Max Marker.   .....

5 Read pages 6–10. Who or what ...

   a   does a bad thing to Mr Duval's boat?   ....

   b   pulls trees up?   ....

   c   crash down on houses?   ....

   d   talks angrily about Max Marker?   ....

   e   says 'Help! Help!'?   ....

6 Read pages 11–15. <u>Underline</u> the right word in *italics*.

    a Max Marker is under the *water/ stones/ trees*.

    b The stones are very *heavy/ light/ small*.

    c The roof crashes down *on/ near/ under* Hannah.

    d Hannah *runs/ stays/ laughs* and helps him.

    e Hannah says 'No' to Max's *money/ friend/ boat*.

    f After that, Max is a *new/ bad/ angry* person.

After you read

  7 Answer the questions. What do you think?

    a Do you like Hannah? Why (not)?

    b Is Max Marker a bad person? Why (not)?

  8 Look at the small picture on page 8. Write the story for that picture: What do Hannah and Mr Duval do in the hurricane? What do they say?

  9 Hannah says 'No' to Max Marker's money. Is she right? What do you think? Is money important to you? Why (not)? Write about it.

10 What do you think? After the hurricane . . .

    a Does Max Marker say 'Sorry' to Mr Duval?

    b Does Max Marker pay for Mr Duval's boat?

    c Are Hannah and Mr Duval friends with Max?

11 Work with a friend. It is after the hurricane. Max Marker is talking to Mr Duval.

    Student A: You are Max Marker. What do you say to Mr Duval?

    Student B: You are Mr Duval. What do you say?

WORD LIST *with example sentences*

cheap (adj) It's not expensive; it's *cheap*.
$10 is cheap but $8 is *cheaper*.

climb (v) Can you *climb* up the tree?

coral reef (n) There's a beautiful *coral reef* under the sea.

crash (v) The driver can't stop, and the car *crashes* into a tree.

everything (pron) Money is important, but it isn't *everything*.

glass-bottomed (adj) In a *glass-bottomed* boat, you can see under the water.

go on (v) The holiday starts today and *goes on* for five days.

help (v) I can't do this. Please *help* me.

hour (n) There are 24 *hours* in a day.

hurricane (n) A lot of trees are down after the *hurricane*.

island (n) Britain, Sicily, Cuba and Hawaii are *islands*.

laugh (v) The children are happy. They're *laughing* and playing.

off (prep/adv) Move your feet *off* the table!

out (prep/adv) Go *out* of the house and into the road.

pay (v) I *pay* £2 for the bus every day.

pull (v) The bad little boy *pulls* his sister's hair.

rich (adj) He's a *rich* man with three houses and a big boat.

roof (n) The rain falls on the *roof* of the house.

stone (n) There are some big *stones* in the river. You can walk across the river on the stones.

wind (n) Listen to the *wind* in the trees.

Pearson Education Limited
Edinburgh Gate, Harlow,
Essex CM20 2JE, England
and Associated Companies throughout the world.

ISBN: 978-1-4058-6947-8

First published 1995
This edition first published 2008

1 3 5 7 9 10 8 6 4 2

Text copyright © Longman Group Ltd 1995
This edition copyright © Pearson Education Ltd 2008

Typeset by Graphicraft Ltd, Hong Kong
Set in 12/20pt Life Roman
Printed in China
SWTC/01

Published by Pearson Education Ltd in association with
Penguin Books Ltd, both companies being subsidiaries of Pearson Plc

For a complete list of the titles available in the Penguin Readers series please write
to your local Pearson Longman office or to: Penguin Readers Marketing Department,
Pearson Education, Edinburgh Gate, Harlow, Essex CM20 2JE, England.

Hannah and the Hurricane

Hannah loves her job on old Mr Duval's small boat. The boat takes people to the beautiful coral reef every day. Then a rich man arrives with a big new boat. Suddenly, there isn't any work for Hannah and Mr Duval. Then the hurricane comes…

Penguin Readers are simplified texts which provide a step-by-step approach to the joys of reading for pleasure.

Series Editors: Andy Hopkins and Jocelyn Potter

Easystarts	**200 headwords**	
Level 1	300 headwords	*Beginner*
Level 2	600 headwords	*Elementary*
Level 3	1200 headwords	*Pre-Intermediate*
Level 4	1700 headwords	*Intermediate*
Level 5	2300 headwords	*Upper-Intermediate*
Level 6	3000 headwords	*Advanced*

Originals   British English

Number of words (excluding activities): 973

Cover illustration by Rod Holt

 Audio CD pack also available

www.penguinreaders.com

ISBN 978-1-405

9 781405